TROPICAL TERRY

JARVIS

FOR JENNA x

WALKER BOOKS
AND SUBSIDIARIES
LONDON · BOSTON · SYDNEY · AUCKLAND

First published 2018 by Walker Books Ltd, 87 Vauxhall Walk, London SE11 5HJ • Text and illustrations © 2018 Jarvis • The right of Jarvis to be identified as author and illustrator of this work has been asserted by him in accordance with the Copyright, Designs and Patents Act 1988 • This book has been typeset in Sutro • Printed in China • All rights reserved. No part of this book may be reproduced, transmitted or stored in an information retrieval system in any form or by any means, graphic, electronic or mechanical, including photocopying, taping and recording, without prior written permission from the publisher. • British Library Cataloguing in Publication Data: a catalogue record for this book is available from the British Library ISBN 978-1-4063-7642-5 (hb) • ISBN 978-1-4063-7862-7 (pb) • www.walker.co.uk • 10 9 8 7 6 5 4 3 2

In Coral Reef City lived some of the most
dazzling shoals of tropical fish
in all the ocean.

Dashing and flashing, they spun and swirled in great flurries of colour.

SWOOSHY SWOOSHY

And then there was ...

Terry.

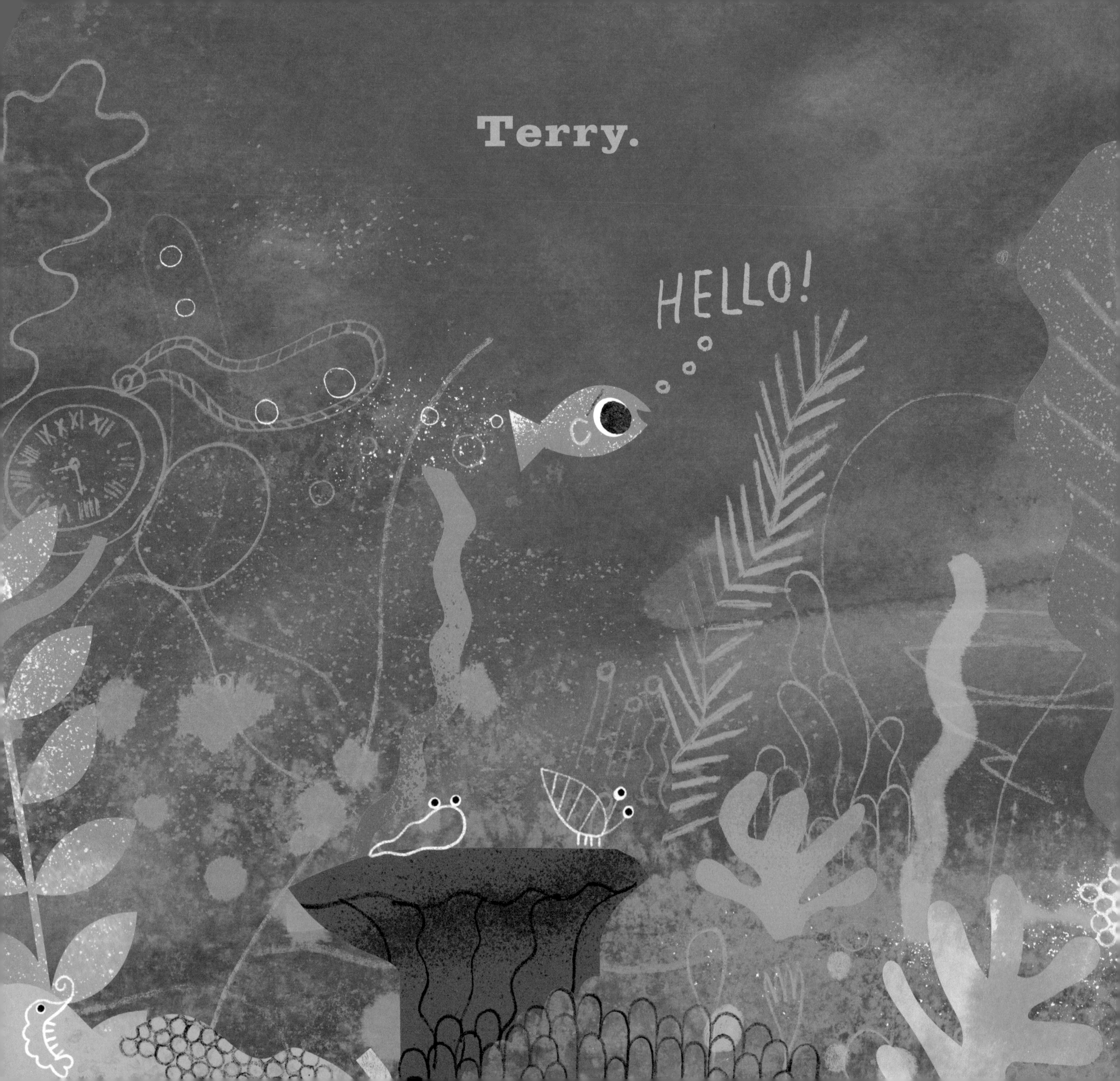

Terry lived with his best friends
Cilla the crab and Steve the sea snail.

Each and every day, the three friends
would play games together –

DODGE-A-DOLPHIN
(Cilla had a great
sidestep) ...

ZIG ZAG

SHARK SPEED

(Steve tried his best) ...

ZOOM

But no matter
how many times Terry asked,
the tropical fish did **NOT** want to play
with him and his friends.

The fancy fish got Terry down in the sea dumps.

"Cheer up, Terry,
you don't need them,"
said Steve.

"You can play with us!"
said Cilla.

OUR
DEEP SEA DEN

But Terry couldn't stop thinking about how he could become part of that dashing, flashing crew.

Then, the next morning, Terry had a brilliant idea.

He gathered as many
bits and bobs as he could find.

And with Cilla and Steve's help
(and a LOT of sticky seaweed),
Terry became...

SNIPPY
SNIPPY

STICKY
STICKY

TROPICAL!

"Hello-o-o-o, everybody!
Just call me
TROPICAL TERRY,"
he bubbled.

Terry was now the most
dazzling tropical fish in ALL of
Coral Reef City.

"Hi, guys," said Terry, casually.

"Wow! Looking good, Terry!" said Long John.

"Do you want to
join us?"
asked Goldy.

"We're going to swim
around in circles!"
grinned Dot.

The new **TROPICAL TERRY** was **SO** popular.
And soon, he was far too busy flaunting and
posing to play with Cilla and Steve.

SWISHY SWISHY

Shimmery and shiny, Terry swirled around and around in circles.

SWOOSHY SWOOSHY

Until...

EDDIE THE EEL arrived in Coral Reef City,

with one thing on his mind ...

DINNER!

And he had a particular taste for big swishy tails and colourful **TROPICAL FISH!**

The tropical fish swam frantically, trying to escape.

But Terry's decorations were slowing him down.

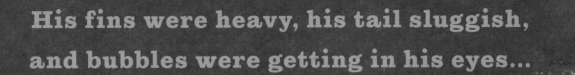

His fins were heavy, his tail sluggish,
and bubbles were getting in his eyes...

Eddie, meanwhile,
was getting closer and closer -
his eyes narrowing,
his jaws opening wider ... and WIDER...

What could Terry do?

"**DODGE** him,
Terry!"
yelled Cilla.

ZIG ZAG

ZOOM

"Quick,
SHARK-SPEED!"
shouted Steve.

And as Terry swerved and dived,
his decorations began to fall off.

The fancy fin,

the swooshy tail...

Suddenly,
Terry knew just
what to do...

HIDE-A-FISH!

Eddie peeped and peered but he couldn't see Terry anywhere. Nobody, you see, was better at hiding than Terry.

OI, FISHY FISHY! WHERE ARE YOU?

So Eddie slithered off to find his dinner elsewhere.

The coast was clear.

"Phew!" gasped Terry.
"If it weren't for Cilla and Steve,
I'd be Eddie's dinner by now!"

And he set off
to find them...

Cilla and Steve were SO glad to see
their friend back to his old self.

"Being tropical just wasn't me,"
said Terry. "Now,
who wants a game of
HIDE-A-FISH?"

OUR
DEEP SEA DEN

"WE DO!"
said all the tropical fish.
"We want to learn how to hide,
just like you, Terry!"

So that's how Terry, Cilla, Steve -
and all the tropical fish -
became friends.

And, guess what?

Eddie the eel had to make do with sand sandwiches for the rest of his days.